HI Hope You Enjoy! ♡3

D0290371

This book belongs to ~~████████~~

How many **Fairy Animals** books have you collected?

- Chloe the Kitten
- Bella the Bunny
- Paddy the Puppy
- Mia the Mouse
- Poppy the Pony
- Hailey the Hedgehog

And there are more magical adventures coming very soon!

Fairy Animals

of Misty Wood

Poppy the Pony

Lily Small

Henry Holt and Company
New York

With special thanks to Thea Bennett

Henry Holt and Company
Publishers since 1866
175 Fifth Avenue
New York, New York 10010
mackids.com

First published in the United States in 2016 by Henry Holt and Company.
Originally published in Great Britain in 2014 by Egmont UK Limited.

Library of Congress Cataloging-in-Publication Data
Names: Small, Lily, author.
Title: Poppy the Pony / Lily Small.
New York : Henry Holt and Company, 2016. |
Series: Fairy animals of Misty Wood | Originally published in Great Britain in 2014 by
Egmont Books Ltd. | Summary: "Poppy the Pony is very shy. She loves soaring through
Misty Wood, but she's too scared to talk to any of the other fairy animals. One day a
thunderstorm comes, and Poppy discovers she is braver than she ever knew. Includes
activities"—Provided by publisher.
Identifiers: LCCN 2016001534 (print) | LCCN 2016027193 (ebook) |
ISBN 978-1-250-13079-2
Subjects: | CYAC: Fairies—Fiction. | Ponies—Fiction. | Animals—Fiction. | Bashfulness—
Fiction. | Friendship—Fiction. | BISAC: JUVENILE FICTION / Fantasy & Magic. |
JUVENILE FICTION / Social Issues / Friendship.
Classification: LCC PZ7.S6385 Po 2016 (print) | LCC PZ7.S6385 (ebook) |
DDC [Fic]—dc23
LC record available at https://lccn.loc.gov/2016001534

Our books may be purchased in bulk for promotional, educational, or business use.
Please contact your local bookseller or the Macmillan Corporate
and Premium Sales Department at (800) 221-7945 ext. 5442
or by e-mail at MacmillanSpecialMarkets@macmillan.com.

First American Edition—2016
Printed in the United States of America by
LSC Communications US, LLC (Lakeside Classic), Harrisonburg, Virginia

1 3 5 7 9 10 8 6 4 2

Contents

CHAPTER ONE

Poppy Needs a Friend

It was a lovely bright morning in
Misty Wood. On top of Sundown
Hill, a little pony called Poppy
was grazing beside her mom.

1

POPPY THE PONY

2

Sundown Hill was the sunniest place in the whole wood. The yellow primroses that grew there shone like sunbeams, and there was plenty of lush green grass, too. Poppy liked the grass very much.

"Yum, yum!" she whinnied as she nibbled the juicy stems. She was nearly full now, but the grass was so tasty she couldn't stop eating.

"That's right, Poppy!" neighed her mom. "We've got lots of work

3

to do today, so you need a big breakfast."

Poppy was a Petal Pony—one of the fairy animals of Misty Wood. Her gleaming coat was the same pale yellow as the primroses and her silky mane and tail were as white as swan feathers. It was the Petal Ponies' special job to swish their glossy tails and waft the beautiful scent of the flowers through the wood. The sweet smells

made all the other animals feel
happy.

"*Woof, woof!*" Loud barking
rang out across the hill.

Poppy stopped chewing and
turned to see who it was.

"Let's have a race!" a voice
called. "I bet I win. *Woof!*"

Poppy heard the patter of
paws on the ground. Lots of paws!
Her long legs started to tremble
as a pack of Pollen Puppies came

scampering through the tall grass.

"*Woof!*" they barked as they
charged along with their tails
wagging. "Hello, Petal Pony.
Woof, woof!"

But instead of answering, all
Poppy could think was *Help!*

You see, Poppy was a very
shy pony, and she found it hard
to talk to fairy animals she didn't
know. Quick as a flash, she
unfurled her sky-blue wings

6

and flew behind her mom to hide.

"Hey, Petal Pony!" barked one of the puppies. "Where did you go?" He peeped through the silky fronds of Poppy's mom's long tail. When he saw Poppy hiding, he trotted around to speak to her.

"There you are," he said with a grin. "We're having a race to Honeydew Meadow. Would you like to come with us?"

Poppy shook her head.

POPPY THE PONY

"Why don't you, Poppy?" said her mom. "You're really good at galloping."

"Yes, you could win the race," barked the puppy. "Come on!"

Poppy hid her face in her long white mane. She felt so shy, she didn't know what to do.

Poppy's mom looked at her kindly. "It'll be fun," she said.

Poppy thought for a moment. Her legs were a lot longer than a puppy's. And she did love to gallop fast. . . .

"Poppy?" Her mom gave her a nudge with her velvety nose. "What do you say?"

Poppy took a deep breath. She wanted to say, "Yes, please. I'd love to!" But her throat went tight and all that came out was a little snuffling noise that sounded like: "*Hm-hm-hm.*"

The puppy wagged his tail.

10

"What did you say? Are you coming?"

Poppy hung her head. She was so embarrassed she felt hot all over.

Poppy's mom looked at her, waiting for her to say something, but Poppy's voice had completely disappeared.

"Maybe not today," Poppy's mom told the puppy. "But thank you very much for asking."

"That's okay! Poppy can play

anytime." The puppy waved a paw at Poppy to say good-bye. "Come on, puppies, let's go!"

The puppies scampered away over the hill, barking happily.

"I wish I could have gone

with them," Poppy sighed. "But I'm so shy I can't even speak to anybody."

Her mom nuzzled her neck. "You have to try to be a bit braver, Poppy. How will the other animals know that you want to be friends if you don't talk to them?" She lifted her head and gazed down the hill at the rest of Misty Wood. "Never mind now—it's time to start work," she said. "The sun's shining and all the flowers are blooming."

Poppy's face brightened. She loved swishing the lovely flower smells around the wood.

Her mom looked thoughtful for a second. "Why don't we split up and go to different places today?" she said. "I'll go to Bluebell Glade. You could start at Heather Hill. There'll be lots of gorgeous heather blossoms there."

"I'd rather be with you,"

14

Poppy said, her tail drooping. She'd never gone without her mom before.

"You'll be fine," her mom told her gently. "And maybe other fairy animals will come and talk to you. You might make a friend."

"Maybe," said Poppy, but she didn't think so. How could she make a friend if all she managed to say was *hm-hm-hm*?

"Just give it a try!" her mom said. "Have a lovely day and I'll see

15

you at supper." She nuzzled Poppy with her nose and then galloped off a little way before opening her wings and soaring into the sky.

Poppy felt a bit lonely, left behind on Sundown Hill. But the sun was shining and she had lots of work to do, so she shook out her white mane, fluttered her wings, and headed off.

Misty Wood looked beautiful as she flew over it. When she arrived

16

at Heather Hill, she heard a loud
buzzing. Hundreds of bumblebees
were hovering over the purple
heather flowers.

Poppy landed in a quiet spot
at the side of the hill and began
flicking her snowy-white tail over
the flowers. A wonderful sweet smell
like honey filled the air.

"*Mmmmm!*" droned the
bumblebees. They flew up and
began swirling in a huge cloud.

17

Then they zoomed down to collect pollen, buzzing even more loudly.

Poppy smiled as she listened. The bees sounded really happy, and it was all because of her!

It was time to move on and find some more flowers.

Poppy cantered down Heather Hill and into the trees. They formed a beautiful green archway for her to run through. Thin fingers of sunlight beamed through the leaves

POPPY NEEDS A FRIEND

above her, making a pretty golden pattern on the floor.

Poppy felt very content as she raced along. But then, just as she reached a clearing, she saw three large fairy animals with stripy faces and silver wings.

Bark Badgers! Poppy skidded to a halt. They mustn't see her, or they might want to come over and talk. Luckily, she spotted a big honeysuckle bush that she could hide behind. She trotted over to it as quietly as she could.

Poppy peeped through the leaves. The badgers were busy doing their special job, decorating the tree bark.

Poppy watched as one badger scraped his claws over the bark, making a flowing line that looked just like a pony's tail. Another was scratching swirly shapes that made Poppy think of a rushing stream.

The smallest badger was making a
circle with lots of marks inside. When
he'd finished, it looked as if a face
was smiling out from the tree trunk.

That's so clever! thought Poppy.

She noticed that the honeysuckle

bush she was hiding behind was
covered in white flowers with long
yellow stems. She sniffed. The
flowers smelled so lovely—even
sweeter than the heather blossoms.
Careful not to make a sound, she

slowly swung her tail back and forth and the scent began to drift toward the badgers. The smallest one looked around.

"Mmmm," he murmured, "something smells nice!"

Poppy stopped swishing her tail and kept very still. After a minute, the badger turned back to his tree trunk and began to draw a new pattern with his claws.

"Phew!" Poppy breathed a

24

sigh of relief. He hadn't seen her.

The badgers smiled as they sniffed the honeysuckle perfume. One by one, they began carving beautiful pictures of flowers on their trees. They looked so happy. Poppy's work was done.

She started creeping away from the clearing . . . but the smallest badger looked around again. And this time he spotted her!

"Hello," he called, twirling his silver whiskers in greeting.

Poppy wanted to hide, but she was so shy she couldn't move an inch.

The badger smiled. "You're a Petal Pony."

Poppy nodded. She tried to say something, but nothing came out. It was as if all the words inside her had run away.

"Thank you for making

everything smell so good," the badger said.

Poppy swallowed. She *had* to say something!

"You're welcome," she whispered very quietly.

The badger waited, but Poppy couldn't say anything else.

"Well—thanks again," he said with a friendly wave of his paw, and he turned back to his friends.

Poppy's head fell. The three

badgers were having so much fun, chatting and laughing as they made their beautiful patterns. If only she could go and join in.

"I'll never, ever be able to make a friend," she whispered to herself. A silvery tear ran down her primrose cheek and dripped off the end of her velvety nose.

29

CHAPTER TWO

The Bluebirds' Song

Poppy shook the tears from her
eyes and began to trot through the
bright green ferns that grew
in clusters beneath the trees.

She couldn't keep feeling sad—she had to find some more flowers. Suddenly, she spotted something ahead. It looked like a huge mirror, shining brightly on the ground.

"Moonshine Pond!" Poppy neighed. "And it's daytime, so the Moonbeam Moles will all be fast asleep. At least I won't have to worry about bumping into any of them."

The Moonbeam Moles lived in burrows on the banks of the pond.

31

Their special job was to catch moonbeams and place them in the water to make it glow like a beautiful pearl. Of course, the moles could only collect moonbeams after dark, so they woke up at night and went to bed during the day. Right now they would all be tucked in, fast asleep in their burrows.

Poppy cantered up to the pond. It was very quiet there. The only thing that moved was Poppy's reflection. Her yellow coat and long white mane looked pretty in the gleaming water.

Not far from the pond, Poppy could see little heaps of earth that marked the entrances to the moles' burrows. She went over and bent her head to see if she could hear the moles inside.

A funny grunting and whistling noise was coming up from under the ground.

"*Och, och, phweee . . .*"

"*Phwee, och, och . . .*"

The moles were snoring! They certainly wouldn't disturb her while she did her work.

Poppy saw some lavender bushes close by. She trotted over and swung her long tail to and fro over the lilac flowers.

"*Aaaah!*" she heard the moles sigh. "*Mmmmm!*" they breathed as the soothing lavender scent reached their sleepy noses, deep underground.

Poppy smiled. Her work at Moonshine Pond was finished. She flicked her wings and soared up through the trees, heading for the Heart of Misty Wood.

Soon she came to a place where the trees grew very tall. Beneath the trees was a grassy glade, and Poppy drifted toward it. As she landed, the grass felt as soft as a cushion under her hooves.

High above in the treetops, Poppy heard the flutter of wings. She looked up. Two bluebirds had landed on a branch.

"*Tweet-tweet*," sang one, flicking his bright blue tail.

"*Cheep-cheep*," replied the other, nodding her little blue head.

Poppy pricked her ears to listen to their lovely song. But they were so high up it sounded very faint. If only they would come closer.

Then Poppy had an idea. She walked over to a rose bush that was growing at the edge of the glade. She brushed her tail over the velvety pink petals, and a beautiful scent rolled like mist across the glade.

One of the bluebirds looked down, his head tilted to the side.

Poppy swept her tail over the roses again.

"*Twee-ee-eet!*" sang the bluebird as the perfume drifted up to him. He leaped off the branch and flew down to the grass.

"*Chee-ee-eep!*" trilled his mate as she joined him.

The two birds hopped around and fluttered their blue wings as if they were dancing. They hadn't noticed Poppy.

They like the smell of roses, Poppy thought with a smile.

There was a rustle at the edge of the glade and a shiny brown nose peeped through a cluster of ferns. A Stardust Squirrel with wings as bright as starshine emerged. Poppy darted behind some trees so he wouldn't see her. But then a voice spoke up on the other side of the nearest tree trunk.

"Ho hum, tiddly-pum! Just look at all these leaves . . ."

Poppy peeped around the tree

trunk. A Hedgerow Hedgehog was rolling around on the ground, collecting dead leaves on her spines.

"*Tweet-tweet! Cheep-cheeep!*" warbled the bluebirds.

"What a lovely song!" the hedgehog sighed. "I think I'll take a break." She sat down to listen. She still had leaves stuck all over her back like a coat.

Who's going to turn up next? thought Poppy. She made herself as small as she could so the hedgehog wouldn't notice her.

"*Tweety-tweet-cheep!*" trilled the bluebirds.

Now Poppy could hear rustling noises all around her. She felt her heart beating fast. There were fairy animals everywhere, making their way into the glade. A herd of Dream Deer trotted past, lifting their graceful heads as they sniffed the roses. Some Bark Badgers pushed their stripy faces through the ferns to watch the birds. Pollen Puppies, tails wagging, flopped on the ground to listen.

More and more animals arrived. Cobweb Kittens floated down through the air. Moss Mice and Holly Hamsters fluttered out from behind the trees, their tiny wings twinkling.

"*Tweeety-tweet! Cheepy-cheep!*" sang the bluebirds.

"Ah, what a wonderful song," a Bark Badger murmured. "And it smells so *lovely* here."

"Shhh," squeaked a little Moss Mouse, swinging from a grass stem. "Just listen!"

All the animals fell silent. As they listened to the bluebirds, Poppy saw her chance. She flicked her wings and flew away from the glade. Thank goodness no one had noticed her!

Poppy flew swiftly through the wood. She was just beginning to feel tired when she saw a gnarled old tree with juicy golden pears hanging from its branches. It had been a long time since breakfast and she was feeling very hungry, so she swooped down and landed under the tree.

She was just about to take a bite from one of the fallen pears when she heard a voice from above.

"Help!" the voice squeaked.

Poppy froze. Someone was in the tree and they were calling to her! But what was she going to do?

CHAPTER THREE

Poppy to the Rescue!

Everything went quiet. Poppy
was just wondering whether she'd
imagined the voice when she heard
it again.

"Help!" it cried. "Please help me!"

Poppy was puzzled. She hadn't seen anyone at all when she flew over the pear tree.

"Who are you?" she tried to say, but her voice wasn't working again and all that came out was "*Hm-hm-hm?*"

"I'm stuck!" the voice whimpered. "Please help me."

Whoever it was sounded very scared.

Poppy peered up. A tiny
Cobweb Kitten, with fur the color
of chocolate, was clinging to a high
branch.

"Please! I want to get down," the kitten meowed, letting go of the branch and waving her paws at Poppy.

Poppy was amazed. The kitten wasn't holding on—so why hadn't she fallen out of the tree? Then Poppy saw that one of the kitten's golden wings was trapped.

Poppy felt so sorry for the kitten that she forgot all about being shy. "You poor thing," she neighed. "Of course I'll help you get down."

"Oh, thank you!"

"What's your name? And how did you get stuck up there?" Poppy called. Her voice was working perfectly now—she didn't even have to think about it.

The kitten was trembling. "My name's Coco," she meowed. "What's yours?"

"Poppy," Poppy replied.

"Hello, Poppy. I was just on my way to meet my friends for a picnic when I spotted these juicy pears."

Poppy nodded. "They do look delicious."

"I thought they'd be perfect for the picnic," Coco said. "I swooped down to pick one, but then my wing got caught."

Poppy tossed her white mane. Then, with a swirl of her shimmering wings, she flew up to the branch. But as soon as she landed, Poppy realized she couldn't reach Coco with her nose. There were too many twigs and leaves in the way.

"Please be quick!" Coco pleaded. "My wing is getting sore."

Carefully, Poppy turned and twirled her tail over Coco's wing, twisting it gently until it came free.

Coco leaped off the branch . . . then squealed with fright.

Poppy saw Coco tumbling down! She flapped her wings hard and flew after her. When she was close enough, she flicked out her tail as far as it would go and managed to catch Coco just before she hit the ground.

"Thank you so much!" Coco gasped as Poppy lowered her onto the grass. "My wing isn't working properly. I can't fly."

A tear welled in Coco's eye.

POPPY TO THE RESCUE!

"And if I can't fly, I'll never get to the picnic in time."

The little kitten looked so sad that Poppy didn't stop to think. "I could take you there if you like," she said in a very soft voice.

Coco was so pleased she jumped up and down. "Ouch!" she squeaked as she tried to flutter her wings. "I must remember not to do that. Thank you, Poppy!"

"You're welcome," Poppy said.

Coco was being so bouncy it made Poppy feel shy again, so she didn't say anything else. She wrapped her tail around the kitten and lifted her onto her back.

"Ooh, this is so much fun!" Coco meowed, holding on to Poppy's coat with her paws. "I've always wondered what it must be like to be a Petal Pony—to gallop so fast and fly so high. Now I'm going to find out!"

Poppy tossed her head. She couldn't help feeling a little bit proud that Coco might want to be like her. "Let's go!" she neighed.

Coco told Poppy that the picnic was happening near Dewdrop Spring. Poppy set off through the trees at a smooth trot. Soon they came out into Honeydew Meadow.

"Could we go a bit faster?" asked Coco.

"Are you sure?" Poppy said.

"I don't want you to fall off."

"I'll hold on tight, I promise," Coco said.

Poppy stretched out her neck

and began to race across the golden flowers.

"Wheeee!" Coco squealed as Poppy leaped over a fallen log. "Woo-hooo!" she whooped as Poppy kicked up her heels and jumped over a hedge.

Poppy's hooves thundered across the golden meadow. When she couldn't gallop any faster, she unfurled her wings and soared into the air.

"Oooooh!" Coco meowed.

Poppy felt the little kitten clinging to her mane as they floated high over a hill where lots of green bushes grew.

"Those are the Mulberry Bushes," Poppy said. "That's where the Misty Wood Rabbit Warren is."

"We're nearly there, then!" squeaked Coco. "Dewdrop Spring runs right by the rabbit warren. Look, there are my friends!"

63

Poppy glanced down. She could see the silvery thread of Dewdrop Spring winding its way past the warren. Then she saw three fairy animals spreading out a picnic blanket made of moss on the banks of the spring. There was a Bud Bunny, a Moss Mouse, and a Holly Hamster.

Poppy's wings began to tremble. It was okay being with Coco. It was easy talking to just one little kitten. But what would happen if she had to meet three new fairy animals all at once?

CHAPTER FOUR

Picnic Time!

Poppy's heart pounded as she glided toward Dewdrop Spring.

"Hey—look at meeee!" Coco called to her friends down below.

The three fairy animals were very surprised indeed when they looked up and saw Coco on Poppy's back.

"How did you get to ride on a Petal Pony?" squeaked the Moss Mouse.

"That looks like fun!" chuckled the Bud Bunny.

"Come down and start the picnic! I'm starving!" shouted the Holly Hamster, rubbing his furry tummy.

Poppy's blue wings glimmered as she circled in the air, looking for somewhere to land. She felt very shy with all of Coco's friends watching her.

Next to the picnic spot there was a grassy bank covered with bright yellow buttercups. Poppy fluttered down toward it.

"I'll drop you here, Coco," she whinnied. As soon as her hooves touched the ground, she carefully lifted Coco down with her tail.

"I've got to go now," she explained

hurriedly. "I've got loads of work to

do and—"

But it was too late.

The Bud Bunny came

hopping toward them through the

buttercups. "Coco—who's your

friend?" she asked.

Poppy hid her face in her

mane. If only she'd flown away

more quickly!

Then the Moss Mouse scampered up, his long whiskers twitching. "Are you all right, Coco?"

"I got stuck in a tree!" Coco explained. "I was trying to pick some pears for our picnic, but my wing got caught. It was horrible." Coco's tail fluffed up like a feather duster at the thought.

"That sounds awful. Oh, look, here comes hungry Harry!" said

the bunny as the Holly Hamster

trotted up on his chubby little legs.

"Who said pears? Did you say

pears?" he said to Coco, puffing

out his cheeks. "I love pears. Did

you bring some?"

Coco shook her head. "No, I was too scared to pick any. I thought I'd be stuck up there forever."

"How did you escape?" asked the mouse.

"Poppy rescued me," Coco purred. "She's amazing!" The kitten twined herself around Poppy's legs, rubbing them with her soft fur as she told her friends how the pony had freed her from the tree.

Coco's friends all looked at Poppy in admiration.

"I'm Max," squeaked the Moss Mouse, standing as tall as he could on his back legs and twirling his whiskers at Poppy.

"I'm Bobbi," said the Bud Bunny, twitching her velvety pink nose.

"And I'm hungry—*starving* hungry!" said Harry.

Poppy looked down at the

buttercups and tried to pretend that she wasn't really there. Her heart was beating so fast, and she felt too hot. If only they would all stop staring at her!

Harry looked longingly over at the picnic blanket. "Let's eat before my tummy gets so empty it starts to cry!" he groaned.

They all turned to the picnic. Poppy was relieved. Finally, she had a chance to escape. She spread her wings, ready to take off. But just then, Max looked back.

"Don't go!" he cried when he saw her.

Poppy opened her mouth and tried to speak, but all that came out was, "*Hm-hm-hm!*"

Coco padded over and rubbed against Poppy's legs again. "You must come to our picnic," she purred.

"Please stay, Poppy!" Bobbi said.

"If you don't all hurry up, I am going to faint from starvation!" Harry called, sucking his cheeks in as thin as they would go—which wasn't very thin at all.

It was no good. Poppy's voice had disappeared again, and she didn't want to seem rude. All she could do was fold her wings back down and trot after the others to the picnic spot.

The mossy blanket was covered

with conker-shell bowls full of nuts
and seeds, bunches of tasty carrots
with leafy green tops, and a basket
of beautiful rosy apples.

Coco, Bobbi, Max, and Harry
settled down and started eating.
But Poppy felt much too shy to
sit down with them. So she stood
behind, shifting nervously from
hoof to hoof. She was very glad
that they were all too busy enjoying
the food to notice her.

79

If I went back to the buttercup patch, she thought, *I could wave my tail over the flowers to spread the perfume. Everyone would be happy, and they'd forget all about me.*

She was just about to slip away when Coco looked around. "Would you like an apple?" she asked.

Before Poppy could even try to answer, the little kitten came padding over with a shiny red

apple in her mouth. She put it
down in front of Poppy.

Poppy licked the apple, but
she didn't bite into it. If she made

a loud crunching noise, everyone
would look at her again.

"Oooh!" squealed Coco
suddenly. "What was that?" She
wiped at her head with her paw.

Poppy felt a fat drop of water
plop onto her mane.

Everyone looked up. The sun
had disappeared, and a big black
cloud was filling up the sky. It was
starting to rain!

"Oh no!" squeaked Max,

holding a carrot over his head as the drops began falling thick and fast. "Our picnic will be ruined!"

CHAPTER FIVE

Under the Oak Tree

"I'm getting wet," meowed Coco,
shaking raindrops out of her fur.

"Me too," squeaked Max.

"We'd better get out of here."

84

"Never mind about getting wet—what about the food?" Harry cried. He started scampering about, gathering all the food in the middle of the mossy blanket. Then he folded the corners together and tied them tightly in a knot.

"Where can we go?" asked Bobbi, flicking the rain from her floppy ears. "There's no shelter here."

The rain was coming down

really hard now. *At least it will make the flowers grow*, Poppy thought.

But she felt very sorry for the four friends. Their picnic was spoiled and they were going to get soaked. If she was brave enough, maybe she could help . . .

She took a deep breath. "Jump on my back!" she whinnied. As soon as the words burst from her mouth, she felt so shy she had to look down at her hooves.

"Really, Poppy?" said Bobbi, her eyes shining.

"Come on, quick!" said Coco, scampering up Poppy's tail and onto her back.

Bobbi did a giant hop and landed just behind Coco.

Harry and Max fluttered their little wings and floated up to join the others. "Don't forget the food!" Harry shrieked.

"I won't," Poppy said. "Hold

on tight!" She picked up the blanket
bundle with her mouth and started
cantering away from Dewdrop
Spring.

"Wheeee!" squealed Coco.

"Isn't this fun?"

"Bouncing bunnies!" cried

Bobbi. "It's brilliant!"

Poppy's tail streamed behind her as she galloped toward the trees. She knew just where to go. Right in the heart of the wood grew a tall oak tree with wide, leafy branches big enough to cover them all.

As soon as she spotted the tree, she slowed down to a gentle trot.

"This is perfect! We'll be dry here," squeaked Max as Poppy came to a halt.

90

Poppy carefully placed the blanket of food on the ground under the tree. Max and Harry fluttered down, and Bobbi and Coco both reached the ground in one big leap.

"Thank you, Poppy," said Harry as he untied the blanket with his front teeth. "I was saving the biggest apple for me, but you can have it. You deserve it!"

This time, Poppy was so glad

Coco's friends were happy that she didn't feel shy or embarrassed. She just took a bite out of the juicy apple and kept on crunching until it was all gone. When she'd finished, she noticed that Coco had disappeared.

"Where's Coco?" she asked.

"I'm here!" purred Coco, scampering up to Poppy with a bunch of daisies. "Lie down, Poppy, and shut your eyes—I'm going to give you a wonderful surprise."

Poppy lay down with her legs folded underneath her. She closed her eyes. She could feel Coco playing with her mane—it was lovely. Her whole body relaxed.

Finally, Coco tapped Poppy on the nose. "Okay—ready!"

When Poppy opened her eyes, she saw that Coco had woven a daisy chain into her mane. The little flowers looked like yellow and white jewels.

"Thank you!" she whinnied. "It's so pretty!"

"Thank *you*," replied Coco.

"You saved us from getting soaking wet. That rain is heavy—listen."

Poppy pricked her ears. *Pit-a-pat, pit-a-pat* went the raindrops as they sploshed on the leaves of the oak tree.

Suddenly, there was a loud *CRACK!* from high up in the sky.

"Uh-oh!" Bobbi cried. "A thunderstorm!"

"Help!" squealed Harry. He covered his ears with his paws.

"I'm scared," whispered Max as another *CRACK!* echoed through the sky.

"It's all right," said Poppy. "Hide under my mane, you two little ones. You'll be safe there."

"Wh-wh-what about all the f-f-f-food?" Harry stammered as he and Max snuggled under Poppy's mane. "What if it gets struck by lightning?"

"It won't," Poppy said calmly

as she gathered the remains of the picnic toward her with her tail. Coco and Bobbi cuddled up next to her tummy. Poppy felt very brave and strong as she swooshed her tail around to hug them close.

BOOM! went the thunder. Poppy could feel Max and Harry trembling. Coco and Bobbi were shivering, too. What could she do to make them forget about the thunder? Then she had an idea.

She'd have to be very brave indeed,

but maybe it would work. . . .

Poppy took a deep breath.

"Shall I tell you a story?" she

asked. She gave a small sigh of relief. Her voice was still working!

"Yes, please!" said Bobbi.

Poppy cleared her throat. "Once upon a time," she began in a strong, clear voice, "there was a baby Petal Pony called Pearl. Her legs were so wobbly she couldn't stand up."

"Why were they wobbly?" asked Max.

"Because she was only one

hour old, and she hadn't learned how to walk yet," said Poppy. "It's quite hard to get the hang of walking when your legs are as long as a Petal Pony's."

"I'd be very scared if that was me," Harry said.

"Pearl wasn't *too* scared, because her mom was with her," Poppy said, "and her mom was very nice and kind. 'Come on, Pearl—you can do it,' her mom said. So Pearl put her front hooves on the ground and pushed until she was halfway up, and . . ."

BOOM! went the thunder. All the animals cowered back against Poppy.

"What happened next?" Coco asked in a shaky voice.

"Pearl pushed and pushed with her hooves, but her legs were still too wobbly. Bump—down she fell again," said Poppy.

101

"Poor little Pearl," said Bobbi. "I hope there's a happy ending for her."

"So do I!" said a gruff voice, and a Bark Badger pushed his stripy face through the bushes.

Then a graceful Dream Deer stepped out from behind the tree. "I'm sure there is," she said in a soft, soothing voice. "But we'll have to hear the rest of the story to find out. . . ."

Now there were rustling noises from all around. Lots of fairy animals were coming under the oak tree to take shelter from the rain. There were Stardust Squirrels and Hedgerow Hedgehogs, Bud Bunnies and Pollen Puppies—and they were all looking at Poppy and waiting for her to continue her story.

There were so many of them that Poppy began to feel a little

shy again. What would she do if her voice stopped working and she couldn't tell the rest of the story?

She spotted a patch of pansies growing from the roots of the oak tree. She swished her tail softly over the purple flowers, and a soothing perfume drifted out.

"Mmm!" sighed Max as he climbed out from under Poppy's mane. "That smells nice. I'm not a bit frightened of the thunder now."

All the fairy animals who had gathered around were looking calm and happy, too.

Poppy went on. "Pearl's mom said: 'Come on, Pearl, you can do it,' and she nudged Pearl with her nose. 'I can't!' said Pearl. 'My legs won't work!' 'They will,' said Pearl's mom. 'You've just got to believe.'"

Poppy paused for a moment. She looked around at all the animals. Their eyes shone as they waited to hear what happened next to baby Pearl. They'd forgotten all about the thunderstorm.

"Pearl stretched out her front legs," Poppy continued. "'I *can* stand up!' she said, and she pushed and she pushed until she was almost up, but then her legs started wobbling again. . . ."

A whisper went up from the animals: "*Come on, baby Pearl! You can do it!*"

"Pearl's mom reached out with her nose and she pushed against Pearl's tail so she didn't fall over again—and suddenly, Pearl was standing up!"

"Hooray!" cried the animals.

"Baby Pearl took one wobbly step, and then she took another. Then Pearl's mom trotted away!"

"No!" squeaked Max. "What did Pearl do?"

Poppy smiled at him and

carried on with the story. "'Don't go without me!' Pearl whinnied. And suddenly she found that her legs were working! Faster and faster they went—until she was galloping after her mom! 'I *can* do it!' Pearl neighed as she cantered along at her mom's side. 'Yes, you can,' her mom said. 'And one day, you'll be the fastest Petal Pony in Misty Wood.' The end!" said Poppy.

"Yay!" A big cheer went up
from all the animals.

They liked her story! Poppy
tossed her head and flicked her long
mane with its pretty daisy chain.

And the strangest thing was that although everyone was looking at her, Poppy didn't feel the slightest bit shy.

CHAPTER SIX

Surprise!

Max fluttered his wings and flew
beside Poppy's head. "Was that story
really about you?" he whispered.

"Yes," Poppy whispered back.
"My mom helped me to stand up

when I was a baby. And one day, maybe I'll be the fastest pony in Misty Wood!"

"I bet you will," said Max.

"The rain's stopped," said Coco, looking up at the top of the oak tree. "The storm's over!" The little Cobweb Kitten fluttered her wings and flew back and forth over the ferns. "My wing's healed!" she called. "Your story made me feel better, Poppy!"

Poppy swished her tail and neighed happily. Lots of other animals started coming over to talk to her. Poppy jumped to her feet, but there was nothing to be shy about. Everyone just wanted to be friendly.

"Your mane would make a great bark pattern," said one of the Bark Badgers. "Come and pose for us sometime. Maybe you could tell us another story—and make

114

everything smell lovely and sweet again?"

"Come around and visit us for snacks!" said a Stardust Squirrel. "We've got some tasty hazelnuts!"

"Hazelnuts? Who said hazelnuts?" Harry cried.

"*Woof! Woof!*" barked a Pollen Puppy. "How about a game of chase? Whenever you like, we'll be ready! *Woof!*"

A Dream Deer blinked shyly

115

at Poppy. "Would you like to come running through the woods with us?" she murmured. "You could spread the flower smells and tell us a story while we go!"

Max's whiskers were twitching again. "I was just thinking," he squeaked. "You might be tired after all that running around and storytelling. Drop by my burrow and we'll make you a big comfy moss cushion to lie on."

"I would love that! Thank you," said Poppy.

Golden shafts of sunlight were shimmering through the branches now. The leaves and ferns of Misty Wood looked so fresh and green. All that was missing was the sweet smell of flowers. The rain had washed it away! It was time for Poppy to get going.

"I'll come and visit you all," Poppy said to her new friends. "And we'll have loads of fun. But first I've got my special job to do. Good-bye for now—and I'll see all of you very soon!"

As the fairy animals called their good-byes, Poppy twirled her blue wings and floated away through the trees. The leafy branches were covered in dazzling raindrops that glinted in the sunlight, and a rainbow twinkled softly in the sky.

SURPRISE!

Poppy glided down and swished her tail over the bluebells and buttercups, roses and lilies, until Misty Wood was filled with the sweetest smells once again. Finally, as the sky was turning pink and the sun began to fade, she galloped back to Sundown Hill.

Her mom was waiting for her, looking worried. "There you are, Poppy!" she neighed. "Did you get caught in the rain?"

Poppy blew on her mom's nose to say hello. "I was fine," she said. "The thunder was very loud, though."

"It was," Poppy's mom said with a shiver. "I was worried about you, all on your own in the storm."

Poppy was about to explain what had happened when there was a flicker of wings close by. It was Max!

"Hello, Poppy," he squeaked as

he fluttered past. "Don't forget to come and get your pony-sized moss cushion!"

Poppy's mom's eyes opened wide with surprise, but before she could say anything, a Bark Badger came trundling through the grass.

"See you soon!" he called to Poppy. "Drop by anytime!"

"Poppy! What's going on?" asked her mom.

Poppy was just about to answer

when a Dream Deer strolled past.
"Can't wait to go running with
you!" the deer called softly.

Then a Pollen Puppy bounced
up. "See you soon for our game
of chase," he yelped, and then
scampered away.

"Well!" Poppy's mom said with
a smile. "You *have* been busy, Poppy.
Very busy indeed!" She nuzzled
Poppy's neck. "And what's this lovely
daisy chain doing in your mane?"

Poppy felt her heart swell as she thought of all the fairy animals she had met that day. Her first-ever friends! There was no need to be shy after all.

"A *friend* made it for me!" Poppy told her mom, who looked as pleased as Poppy felt.

Then Poppy kicked up her heels, neighed with joy, and cantered off to find a tasty patch of grass for her supper.

125

Turn the page for

lots of fun

Misty Wood

activities!

Picnic Time!

In the story, Poppy's new friends have a delicious picnic with lots of tasty treats for everyone.

What are your favorite things to eat at a picnic? Write them down on the next page.

1. CuPcake
2. Berries
3. Straberry→
4. apple
5.
6.
7.
8.

Draw the treats from your list on page 129 on the picnic blanket.

Connect the Dots

Follow the numbers and connect
all the dots to make a lovely picture
from the story.

Start with dot number 1. When
you've connected all the dots,
try drawing Poppy's new friends
around her!

Fairy Animals
of misty Wood

Hailey the Hedgehog

Lily Small

Henry Holt and Company
New York

With special thanks to Liss Norton

Henry Holt and Company
Publishers since 1866
175 Fifth Avenue
New York, New York 10010
mackids.com

First published in the United States in 2016 by Henry Holt and Company.
Originally published in Great Britain in 2013 by Egmont UK Limited.

Library of Congress Cataloging-in-Publication Data
Names: Small, Lily, author.
Title: Hailey the Hedgehog / Lily Small.
New York : Henry Holt and Company, 2016. |
Series: Fairy animals of misty wood | Summary: "A special story for Christmas
introducing Hailey the Hedgerow Hedgehog, the newest addition to the Fairy
Animals of Misty Wood"—Provided by publisher.
Identifiers: LCCN 2015050734 (print) | LCCN 2016023317 (ebook) |
ISBN 978-1-250-13079-2
Subjects: | CYAC: Fairies—Fiction. | Hedgehogs—Fiction. | Forest animals—Fiction. |
Christmas—Fiction. | BISAC: JUVENILE FICTION / Fantasy & Magic. | JUVENILE
FICTION / Social Issues / Friendship.
Classification: LCC PZ7.S6385 Hai 2016 (print) | LCC PZ7.S6385 (ebook) |
DDC [Fic]—dc23
LC record available at https://lccn.loc.gov/2015050734

Our books may be purchased in bulk for promotional, educational, or business use.
Please contact your local bookseller or the Macmillan Corporate
and Premium Sales Department at (800) 221-7945 ext. 5442
or by e-mail at MacmillanSpecialMarkets@macmillan.com.

First American Edition—2016
Printed in the United States of America by
LSC Communications US, LLC (Lakeside Classic), Harrisonburg, Virginia

1 3 5 7 9 10 8 6 4 2

Contents

CHAPTER ONE

Parade Day!

Winter had come to Misty Wood, and the fairy animals were very excited—today was the day of the Christmas Parade!

Hailey, a tiny hedgehog, lay in her cozy bed of moss, listening to the wind outside singing through the trees. She pulled her blanket of velvety dock leaves up to her nose.

"I do love winter," Hailey said with a sigh. As she pictured the wind blowing the last of the golden leaves from the branches and the woods twinkling with frost, she started to smile.

"Are you up, Hailey?" her dad

called from the far end of their
burrow.

"Nearly," Hailey called back.
She jumped out of bed, licked her
tiny pink paws, and gave her face
a quick wash. Then she checked her
dandelion clock. "Yay!" she cried.
"It's breakfast time!"

When she got to the other
end of the burrow, her dad was
busy chopping acorns. "Morning,
Hailey," he said. "I'm making

3

you some acorn porridge to keep you nice and warm out there. The woods are going to need a lot of tidying up before the parade."

"Great!" Hailey exclaimed. "I love having lots of leaves to collect." She fluttered her silver-and-red wings excitedly, sending sparkles of glittering light around the burrow.

Hailey was a Hedgerow Hedgehog. Like all the other fairy animals, she had a special job

4

to do to help make Misty Wood
a wonderful place to live. The
Hedgerow Hedgehogs' job was to
collect fallen leaves on their prickly
spines, to keep the woods neat
and tidy. That was why Hailey
loved winter so much. There were
so many colorful leaves to gather,
especially on a windy day like this.

Dad finished making the
porridge and poured it into three
nutshell bowls. Hailey took hers

5

and went to sit on a pebble stool in the corner. Just as she ate her first mouthful, a gust of cold air came whisking through the burrow.

"It's only me," a voice called. Hailey's mom hurried inside. Her paws were full of mistletoe sprigs. "Goodness!" she exclaimed. "What a wind!" Laying the mistletoe on the conker table, she smoothed down the ruffled fur on her face and legs.

7

"Ooh, is the mistletoe for the Christmas Parade?" Hailey asked. She could hardly wait for the parade to start. It took place every year. All the fairy animals dressed up in beautiful leaves and berries and marched through Misty Wood behind the Moss Mouse pipe-and-drum band. Afterward, everyone visited the nests and burrows of their friends to admire their decorations and to share a tasty

nibble or an acorn cup of warm
cranberry juice.

"Yes," her mom replied. "I'm
using mistletoe and holly this year."
She turned around, and Hailey saw
that her mom's prickles were stuck
all over with shiny red holly berries.

"I'll string them together
to make garlands," her mom
continued. She shook the berries
from her spines and pushed them
into a tidy pile beside the fire.

9

Hailey couldn't stop smiling
as she pictured herself wearing a
beautiful red-and-white garland. In
fact, she was grinning so much that
some porridge trickled out of the
corner of her mouth! Hailey quickly

licked it up with her velvety pink tongue.

"Here's your breakfast," said Hailey's dad, passing her mom a bowl of porridge. "And I'm making my special chestnut pudding for after the parade."

"Yippee!" Hailey cheered. That was another good thing about winter—there were always chestnuts to be found, and Dad's chestnut pudding was *delicious*!

11

Hailey ate her porridge quickly. Every day she made sure that Misty Wood was spick-and-span, but today—parade day—she was determined to be extra careful. Today, she wouldn't leave a single leaf out of place. And she had to make sure she got home earlier than usual, too, so she'd have time to dress up.

"I'm off, then," she said as soon as her bowl was empty.

"Don't forget that the parade begins at one o'clock, Hailey," her mom reminded her.

"I won't," Hailey said with a smile. There was *no way* she was going to miss her favorite event!

Spreading her wings, she fluttered up the long passageway that led out of her warm burrow and into Hawthorn Hedgerows, which grew at the very edge of Misty Wood.

As soon as Hailey got above ground she could see that the wind had been busy. Only a few leaves still clung to the twigs above her head. They fluttered as the wind danced around them, whistling its winter tune.

They'll be off soon, too, thought Hailey, smiling. *And then I'll have even more leaves to tidy.*

She flitted out from under the hedgerow and gasped in delight.

14

Jack Frost had been at work during the night, sprinkling his glittering ice crystals across the grass. The crystals shimmered pink, blue, and silver in the wintry sunshine, and each blade of grass stood up stiff and straight no matter how hard the wind blew.

Hailey gazed around. "*Beautiful,*" she breathed. She fluttered up into the air and spread her wings wide so the wind would lift her high. She

15

wanted to look at the grassy spaces
between the hedgerows. "I'll start
collecting leaves in the messiest
patch," she said to herself.

Up, up, up she soared into
the clear blue sky. Soon, Misty

Wood was spread out beneath her like a colorful patchwork quilt. The frosted grass glinted silver. Dewdrop Spring was the same bright blue as the sky, with spots of shiny ice here and there. And the patch of snowdrops beside it looked as clean and white as a fluffy cloud.

Farther on still, Moonshine Pond shone pearly blue, full of glowing moonbeams, and beyond that was the pretty, vivid purple of Heather Hill.

Right in the center of it all was a patch of deep, dark green—the mysterious Heart of Misty Wood, where the Wise Wishing Owl lived.

Hailey had never seen the Wise Wishing Owl, but she had heard lots of stories about her wisdom. And everyone said that she had the power to grant wishes.

As Hailey looked around, she spotted a patch of leaf-strewn grass not far from her burrow. She quickly fluttered down. "Perfect!" she cried happily, puffing out her spikes. "Now I'm ready to start work!"

CHAPTER TWO

Hungry Hugo!

Tucking her nose and legs in against her tummy and folding her glittering wings, Hailey curled herself into a tight ball. Then she

rolled to and fro across the frosty
grass, gathering the leaves on her
prickles.

Soon the patch of grass was
clear. Hailey scurried over to a

nearby hedge and shook herself.
The leaves fluttered down from
her spines, and she scooped them
into a tidy heap at the base of the
hedge. Smiling, she looked across
the spotless grass. "Good job!" she
congratulated herself. "Now on to
the next one."

She unfurled her wings and
flew farther into the woods.

Soon, she came to a grove
where the Holly Hamsters were

22

hard at work. They were nibbling the glossy holly leaves into their beautiful curved shapes.

"Hello, Holly Hamsters!" Hailey called as she fluttered past.

"Hello, Hailey!" they called back, their chubby cheeks bulging.

Just beyond the holly grove was an ancient chestnut tree with twisted branches and a huge, fat trunk. Leaves were scattered around it, and Hailey eagerly

swooped down to gather them
all up.

As she rolled to and fro,
collecting the leaves, she made
up a little song:

> *I love winter when the wild wind*
> *blows,*
> *Scattering the leaves all around,*
> *all around,*
> *Even though it chills my nose*
> *and toes,*
> *When I roll on the frosty ground.*

Suddenly, she heard a small voice. "I hate winter," it said. "I don't know why you're singing about it. It's the worst season of the whole year!"

Hailey stopped rolling and uncurled herself. She looked around in surprise. How could anybody hate winter?

A teeny-tiny Holly Hamster with pale brown fur and yellow wings was crouched on the edge of the holly grove. His head and wings were drooping miserably. Hailey recognized him—it was Hugo.

"Whatever's the matter, Hugo?" asked Hailey.

"I've ruined my holly bush," he replied, looking up sadly. "And now it's going to look horrible for the Christmas Parade. Every fairy animal in the whole wood will march past here and see what I've done."

Hailey fluttered over to him.

26

"Perhaps it's not as bad as you . . ." She fell silent as she spotted the bush. "Oh, dear."

The bush was almost completely bare, with every leaf nibbled right down to the stem.

Hailey stared at Hugo. "What happened to it?"

"I was hungry," Hugo said. "And the leaves were so yummy I couldn't stop eating them." He peered up at Hailey dreamily. "Honestly, they were the most delicious things I've ever tasted—even more delicious than chestnuts!" He sat back on the ground and gave a loud burp.

Hailey's tummy rumbled as

28

she thought of her dad's chestnut pudding. It was hard to imagine anything tasting nicer. They must have been very tasty leaves indeed!

"Maybe I should try digging up the whole bush," Hugo said. "Then I could hide it." The tiny hamster leaped up and began scratching at the soil around the bush's roots.

"No, Hugo!" Hailey cried. "Don't do that." She rubbed her

29

nose thoughtfully. "I think I know what to do," she said at last.

Hugo looked at her hopefully, his dark eyes shining. "Really?"

"Wait here a moment," said Hailey. She fluttered back to the chestnut tree and quickly rolled over the last of the leaves to stick them to her prickles. Then she whooshed back to Hugo.

"Here you go," she said, shaking the leaves to the ground.

"You can nibble these into holly leaf shapes, and I'll hang them on the bush."

Hugo bounced up and down on his hind legs. "That's brilliant! Thanks, Hailey!" he cried.

"Just make sure you don't gobble them all up this time," Hailey said with a grin.

"I won't," Hugo said, patting his furry tummy. "I'm far too full!" Then he set to work, taking dainty

little bites out of the edges of the
bright chestnut tree leaves.

Hailey twisted the leaf stems
around the holly twigs and soon the
bush was covered in golden holly-
shaped leaves.

"These leaves make my bush look so pretty!" Hugo cried out happily. He hugged Hailey, then leaped back. "Ouch! I forgot all about your prickles!" He chuckled, rubbing his paws.

"Sorry," giggled Hailey. "But I'm glad you're pleased with your *holly* bush."

"I am!" Hugo exclaimed. Then he looked at the little pile of spare leaves next to him. "Can you close

your eyes for a minute?" he asked
Hailey.

"Why?" Hailey said, puzzled.

"I can't tell you yet—it's a
surprise."

Hailey loved surprises. She
closed her eyes and listened, trying
to work out what Hugo was doing.
But all she could hear was the
rustle of leaves.

"Ta-da!" cried Hugo after a
few minutes.

Hailey opened her eyes.

"I made this just for you," Hugo said. He held up a beautiful garland made from all the spare leaves. He slipped it over Hailey's head. "It's to say thank you for helping me."

"It's lovely!" Hailey exclaimed. "Thanks, Hugo. I'll wear it in the Christmas Parade. Ooh, I'd better get going—I've got loads of work to do before then!"

CHAPTER THREE

A Shimmer of Moonbeams

Hailey soared into the air and fluttered quickly over the rabbit warren. Down below, her friend

Bella the Bud Bunny was hard at work opening snowdrop buds with her twitchy nose. Hailey waved, but she didn't fly down to speak to Bella in case it made her late for the parade.

She flew over Dewdrop Spring, then on to Moonshine Pond, which shone like a blue pearl in the winter sunshine. "Ha!" she cried as she spotted some leaves at the pond's edge.

Hailey flew down to land. She curled into a ball and rolled quickly down the bank, gathering the leaves on her prickles as she went. She sang her song as she rolled faster and faster:

I love winter when the wild wind

blows,

Scattering the leaves all around,

all around,

Even though it chills my nose

and toes,

When I roll on the frosty ground.

"I used to love winter, but I most definitely don't anymore!" said a gloomy voice.

The voice was coming from a tall pine tree beside the pond.

Hailey unrolled quickly, and looked around in surprise. "Who said that?" she asked.

"Me, Maisie the Moonbeam Mole," the voice replied softly.

Hailey was very puzzled indeed. Moonbeam Moles didn't usually come out during the day. They did their special job at nighttime— catching moonbeams and scattering them in Moonshine Pond to make it look pearly and beautiful. During

41

the day they stayed in their burrows and slept—and they certainly didn't go climbing trees! Hailey knew that they woke up specially for the Christmas Parade each year—but it was a bit too early yet.

Hailey fluttered over quickly to investigate.

A pair of tiny brown eyes peeked out from among the pine needles. They looked very tired and were full of tears.

"What's wrong, Maisie?" Hailey gasped. "And why are you still awake?"

"I've been here since last night." Maisie sniffed sadly. "My net's caught in this tree, and I can't pull it free." She crept along a branch and pointed up to the top of the tree with a trembling paw.

Hailey saw something glowing among the branches. It was the net—crammed full of twinkling

moonbeams. It had gotten tangled around some pinecones.

"I can't put my moonbeams into the pond"—Maisie gulped—"so it won't look lovely for the Christmas Parade."

"But it *does* look lovely," Hailey told her. "I noticed it when I was flying this way. It looks like a beautiful pearl." She flew up and patted the tiny mole's shoulder, trying to make her feel better.

45

"Not my bit of the pond," sobbed Maisie. She pointed to a patch of water close to the bank. Now Hailey understood why Maisie was so upset. The water there was dark and still, with not even a hint of glistening moonlight.

Hailey thought hard. "I know what to do!" she cried. "I'll hook my prickles through your net. Then I'll be able to fly up and lift it clear of those pinecones."

46

Maisie stopped crying and gazed hopefully at Hailey. "Do you think it will work?" she whispered.

"There's only one way to find out," said Hailey.

She soared to the top of the tree, then fluttered around it, hooking the net over her prickles. "Here goes," she called. Flapping her wings hard, she flew higher still. Part of the net came free and some pinecones dropped to the ground.

"It's working!" squealed Maisie happily.

Hailey flapped her wings harder than ever. More pinecones dropped down and now most of the net was free. "One more try," Hailey panted. Using all of her strength, she zoomed into the air and suddenly the net was dangling free below her. The moonbeams twinkled as they swung from side to side.

"Hurray!" Hailey cheered. She flew to the ground with the heavy net.

Maisie fluttered down beside her, her lilac wings shimmering in the sunshine. "Thank you, thank you," she cried. Her tiny eyes shone with relief as she unhooked the net from Hailey's spines. "Now the pond will look perfect for the parade!"

Scooping out a pawful of

moonbeams, Maisie tossed them into the patch of dark water. They plopped down out of sight, then rose to the surface and their beautiful pearly light rippled out, making the water gleam.

"That looks beautiful, Maisie," breathed Hailey, flying up to see the pond from above.

"All because of you," replied Maisie. She reached into her net and took out the last glowing

moonbeam. "May I give you a
present to thank you for helping
me?" she asked shyly.

51

"Oh yes, please!" Hailey cried. She loved presents!

Maisie placed the moonbeam on the biggest leaf in Hailey's garland. Hailey watched entranced as gold and silver sparkles spread from leaf to leaf. Soon the whole garland was twinkling brightly.

"Thank you!" gasped Hailey, astonished. She'd never seen anything so beautiful before. It was as though she were wearing

a necklace made of glittering
moonlight.

"No, thank *you*, Hailey,"
Maisie said. "If you hadn't helped
me, the pond wouldn't have looked

its best for the Christmas Parade today."

"The parade!" Hailey cried, remembering how much she had to do before it began. "I must go! Bye, Maisie."

CHAPTER FOUR

A Starry Surprise

Hailey fluttered up into the air and headed for the trees that grew in the Heart of Misty Wood. She could see a few untidy leaves on the grass there. As she drew near, she started to sing her winter song:

I love winter when the wild wind

blows—

"Well, I don't!" boomed a cross voice. It was coming from behind a tree at the very back of the Heart of Misty Wood.

Hailey peeped around the tree trunk nervously, wondering who it could be.

Boris, one of the Bark Badgers,

was hunched on the frosty ground.
He was frowning at his paw.

"What's wrong, Boris?" Hailey
asked. The Bark Badgers carved
beautiful patterns into tree trunks
with their strong claws. They were
usually very kind and helpful.
Hailey had never seen one looking
so grumpy before.

"I'm supposed to be carving
wintry patterns into the bark of the
trees around here," Boris replied.

57

"I wanted everything to be perfect for the parade, so I flew up onto a branch to reach farther up the trunk. But the branch was slippery with frost and I fell down." He held up his paw and Hailey saw that it was sore and swollen. "Now my paw's so painful that I can't do my job," he sighed.

"Poor you," Hailey said. She wondered what she could do to help him.

"I should have been more careful!" Boris said glumly. "Now when the parade comes past here, the fairy animals won't be thinking happy, Christmassy thoughts.

They'll be thinking, look at those plain old trees!"

Suddenly, they heard some loud barking and looked around, startled. A group of Pollen Puppies came scampering along, their ears flopping and their tongues hanging out with excitement. "Hey! Aren't you coming to the Christmas Parade?" the puppies woofed, wagging their tails and scattering specks of golden pollen all around.

"Is it time?" Hailey asked them anxiously.

"Nearly," one of the puppies woofed. "And we don't want to be late!"

61

"Neither do I!" Hailey gulped as the playful pups went bounding away. Her mind started whirring. She couldn't leave poor Boris looking so unhappy. Maybe she could help him *and* make it back home in time for the start of the parade. . . .

"Let me help," Hailey said. "My spines are nearly as sharp as a badger's claws. If you tell me what to do, perhaps I can carve the tree trunks for you."

Boris's face broke into a cheery smile. "That would be wonderful!" he exclaimed.

Hailey flew up and pressed her prickles against the first tree. "Okay, I'm ready," she said. "Tell me what to do."

"Go up a bit," called Boris.

Hailey fluttered upward. She felt her spines cutting through the tree's bark. "I think it's working!" she cried excitedly.

"Now right a bit," Boris said, beaming.

Hailey flew right.

"Left, then down," called Boris.

Hailey followed all of Boris's instructions.

"That's it," he said at last. "The first tree's finished. Let's see if it worked."

Hailey turned to look at the tree trunk. "Oh!" she gasped. "How pretty!" Her spines had carved a

pattern of beautiful lacy snowflakes cascading from the sky.

"Next tree!" declared Boris. "Quick!"

Hailey worked at top speed, and soon she'd carved snowflake patterns into all of Boris's trees. "I'd better go home now," she said as she turned to admire the last carved trunk.

"Hold on, there's just one more thing to do," said Boris, holding up a piece of smooth bark that had been gnawed into a diamond shape. Hurriedly, Hailey pressed her spines against it and moved in the directions Boris told her.

"There," he said. "All done." He held up the bark to show Hailey and she saw that she'd carved a beautiful star.

"Lovely!" she exclaimed.

"It's for you," Boris said. "To thank you for all your help." He

hung it right in the middle of her

glowing leaf garland.

"Thank you!" cried Hailey.

"And now I must fly! Bye, Boris."

She made up her mind to go

straight home. "If I stop and pick

up any more leaves, I won't have time to get ready for the parade," she said to herself.

Her red-and-silver wings fluttered furiously as she sped along. She raced past a tree hung with balls of white-berried mistletoe. It reminded her of the decorations her mom was making, and she flapped her wings harder.

Just as she was approaching Dandelion Dell, she spotted some

69

leaves scattered messily on the ground beneath a large oak tree.

"Oh, dear!" Hailey squeaked. The parade would be coming this way, and everyone would see them. *I'll pick them up quickly*, she thought, *then I'll rush straight home. I should still be on time.*

Hurriedly, she flew down, then curled up tight and began to roll this way and that, gathering the leaves. As soon as she started doing her job she stopped worrying about being late and started singing her wintry song again:

> *I love winter when the wild wind*
> *blows,*
> *Scattering the leaves all around,*
> *all around,*
> *Even though it chills my nose*
> *and toes,*
> *When I roll on the frosty ground.*

"How can you sing at a time like this?" a voice called from a branch in the tree high above her.

Hailey stopped singing and uncurled quickly. "A time like what?" she replied, fluttering upward.

"A time as terrible and horrible and awful as this!" the voice wailed.

CHAPTER FIVE

Acorn Disaster!

Hailey flew closer. A beautiful silver
Stardust Squirrel with cute tufty
ears was crouched miserably on a
branch, a broken basket beside her.

"Are you all right?" Hailey asked anxiously.

"No," huffed the squirrel. "I am actually all *wrong*!"

"Oh, dear." Hailey scratched her head with a tiny pink paw. "What's the matter?"

The squirrel sighed and twitched her bushy tail, sending a puff of glittery stardust into the air. "Are you sure you want to know?" she said, looking at Hailey and tilting her head to one side.

Hailey nodded.

"It's a very sad story. It's so sad it might even make you cry."

"Oh, er, that's all right," said Hailey bravely.

"Okay then." The squirrel clasped her front paws together. "Once upon a time, there was a very beautiful Stardust Squirrel called Sabrina—that's me," she added.

Hailey nodded and smiled.

"And one day—today, actually—Sabrina's mommy sent her out to fetch some acorns to decorate the delicious cake that she's making for the Christmas Parade. So Sabrina did as she was told, because as well as being beautiful she's a very good little Stardust Squirrel. She filled her basket right to the brim. But then disaster struck!" Sabrina stared at her basket sadly. "Her basket broke and the acorns went all over the ground." Sabrina looked at Hailey. "Isn't that just the saddest story you've ever heard?"

Hailey nodded solemnly. "Yes, it is a very sad story," she said. "But maybe I can help you give it a happy ending."

Sabrina's eyes lit up. "How?"

Hailey fluttered over and examined the basket. It was woven from stems of dried grass, but some of them had broken and there was a hole in the bottom.

"Let's try putting some leaves over the hole," suggested Hailey.

"That might do the trick." She shook some leaves from her prickles, then carefully pressed a few on the bottom of the basket.

"Ooh, that looks a lot better," Sabrina said, twitching her tail excitedly. "You can't see the hole at all now."

Hailey and Sabrina flew down to the ground. There were acorns scattered all over the grass, and they scampered around, picking them up and dropping them into the basket.

"Here goes," she said, lifting it.

For a moment it looked as though the repair was strong enough, but then the acorns and leaves fell through the hole and rolled across the grass again.

"Oh no!" Sabrina groaned. "Now my story is going to have an even sadder ending than it did before!"

"Don't worry, I know how we can definitely make it happy," Hailey said.

Sabrina frowned at her. "How?"

"I'll collect them with my prickles. I'm sure they'll pick up

81

acorns just as well as they pick up leaves from the ground."

Sabrina looked doubtful. "There's an awful lot of them."

"Well, I've got an awful lot of prickles!" Hailey giggled. She curled into a ball and began to roll. Soon all the acorns were stuck to her prickles, along with the rest of the fallen leaves.

"Come on, let's get these to your mom," Hailey said. "We'll

have to hurry. The parade will be starting soon, and we mustn't miss it."

"Thank you!" Sabrina cried. "Now my story will have a very happy ending indeed!"

They flew at top speed through the trees, dodging between the branches. "There!" said Sabrina at last as a large nest came into view. It was made of sticks, dried grass, and leaves, and it was wedged into the fork where two branches joined the trunk of a tall beech tree. They landed on a large branch.

"If you don't mind, I'll just put the acorns here," said Hailey. "I've got to go home to get ready."

"That will be great," Sabrina replied. "I can easily roll them into our nest from here."

Hailey shook her prickles. A few of the acorns came tumbling off, but most of them stayed put.

"Hang on, I'll get them off,"

said Sabrina. Grabbing an acorn, she pulled with all her might. "I'm not hurting you, am I, Hailey?"

Hailey could feel the tug on her spines but it wasn't sore. "No, it's okay, pull as hard as you can!"

Sabrina pulled and pulled and then, finally . . . *pop!* . . . the acorn came away from Hailey's spine.

"Hurray," cheered Hailey and Sabrina together.

"Now I *know* I'm strong

85

enough to get them off," said
Sabrina proudly. "I'll be as quick
as I can, so you're not late for the
parade." One by one, Sabrina
yanked the acorns from Hailey's

spines. "That's all of them!" she panted at last. "And a good thing, too. I'm puffed out!"

"Phew!" Hailey sighed with relief. "Now I must fly home as *fast* as my wings can take me!"

"Just a minute," Sabrina said as Hailey was about to flutter into the air. Sabrina flew above Hailey and flicked her tail. Twinkling silver stardust showered down on Hailey. "That's to say thank you for helping me," Sabrina said with a smile.

"Wow!" Hailey gasped, twisting her head to look at her spines. They were twinkling like stars. "Thanks, Sabrina. That looks amazing!" Hailey flew up into the air. "See you at the parade," she called as she sped off through the trees. "If I get there in time . . ." she whispered to herself.

CHAPTER SIX

An Unexpected Guest

Hailey flew faster than she'd ever flown before. Misty Wood raced by in a blur, but at last she saw Hawthorn Hedgerows.

Zooming toward the ground,

she saw all the Hedgerow

Hedgehogs outside her burrow.

They were dressed in beautiful

90

garlands made of berries, acorns, and golden leaves, ready for the Christmas Parade.

Hailey's mom and dad were

among them, decked out in bright holly berries and mistletoe. They were looking around the crowd anxiously. Their eyes lit up in relief when they saw Hailey swishing through the air toward them.

"Where have you been?' Hailey's mom asked as she landed.

"Sorry," Hailey panted. "I had to help some friends and it made me late. Do I still have time to get dressed up for the parade?"

Suddenly, Hailey noticed that everyone was staring at her, their mouths gaping in astonishment. She began to feel a tiny bit worried.

"What's wrong?" she asked. She wondered if there was still an acorn or two stuck on her prickles.

"Nothing's wrong," her dad replied. "You look . . ."

"Wonderful!" her mom finished for him.

"Yes, you do," the other

hedgehogs agreed, crowding around to see her better.

Hailey's neighbors Henry and Hilda scurried into their burrow and came back carrying an upturned mushroom cap filled with water that they used as a mirror. "Here," they said, setting it down in front of Hailey. "Take a look at yourself."

Hailey peered at her reflection. "Oh!" she gasped. Looking back at her was a hedgehog whose fur and prickles twinkled with silver stardust. Around her neck she wore a beautiful leafy garland that shone with pearly moonlight. A diamond-shaped piece of bark carved with a five-pointed star hung from it. Hailey stared and stared. She could hardly believe that the reflection was hers.

"That's the best Christmas costume I've ever seen!" Hailey's mom said, giving her a hug.

"We must go!" her dad cried.

"We don't want the parade to start

without us."

The hedgehogs took off, their wings glinting in the wintry sunshine. They flew fast, and soon they spotted Honeydew Meadow below them. A huge crowd of fairy animals was gathering there.

"Hurray!" cried Hailey. "We're not too late after all!"

Hailey, her mom and dad, and all their hedgehog friends fluttered to the ground and landed gently.

The Moss Mouse band was ready and waiting. Each mouse wore a lacy hat nibbled from a scarlet rosehip and, on their tails, a bow made from braided grass. They held their reed pipes and walnut shell drums ready to play. One tiny mouse started beating his drum eagerly as soon as he saw Hailey.

"Not yet, Morris," his mom whispered. "I'll tell you when to play."

"Hello, Moss Mice!" Hailey cried. "You all look so nice!" She could hardly wait for the music to begin.

Hailey's friend Bella the Bunny came hopping over. She was wearing a garland of white snowdrops around each long velvety ear and one around her neck. "Wow, you look fantastic, Hailey!" she cried.

"So do you," said Hailey.

She skipped around in a circle, too excited to keep still for even a moment.

Hailey heard some wings flapping above her head. She looked up eagerly and saw the Stardust Squirrels fluttering down. They were wearing garlands of polished nutshells and their fur shimmered with silver starlight. Hailey saw Sabrina and waved.

"Mom's Christmas cake looks

lovely—thanks to you," Sabrina called out to her.

Hailey grinned and puffed out her spikes proudly.

Next, the Cobweb Kittens arrived, their wings gleaming.

"Look at their costumes!" gasped Bella. The kittens wore garlands woven from glistening cobwebs and hung with bright, glimmering dewdrops.

"Everyone looks wonderful,"

Hailey said happily. "I'm so glad I got here in time."

Then the cheeky Pollen Puppies came scampering over, wagging their tails in excitement. "Whoo-hoo for the Christmas Parade!" they barked in chorus. "Whoo-hoo-woofy-whoo!"

Next, the Bark Badgers came marching past in a line, their silver wings neatly folded. Their black-and-white fur gleamed in the winter sunshine, and they wore garlands made from beautifully carved bark shapes.

"And . . . halt!" cried the badger leader. They all stopped marching, and Hailey noticed Boris right at the back.

"Hi, Boris! How's your paw?" she called.

"Not too bad," he replied. "It won't stop me from being in the parade!"

103

Then the Holly Hamsters arrived. Their golden fur shone brightly, and around their necks they wore garlands of crimson holly berries.

Hugo came trotting over, grinning from ear to ear. "Just wait till everyone sees my holly bush," he whispered. "I bet they've never seen anything like it." His dark eyes widened suddenly. "Gosh," he said, stepping back and gazing at Hailey in astonishment. "You look beautiful, Hailey."

Hailey smiled. "Thanks, Hugo."

Finally, the Moonbeam Moles

105

appeared. They looked sleepy, but very happy to be there. Garlands of moonbeams hung around their necks, glowing like strings of pearls. Hailey looked over at Maisie and waved her paw. Maisie waved back with a snoozy smile.

Suddenly, the crowd fell silent. Hailey heard a gentle rustle from somewhere behind her. Turning, she saw an enormous bird flying toward Honeydew Meadow from

the Heart of Misty Wood. The
bird had huge feathery wings that
glinted gold in the sunshine. Her
brown eyes were big and round and
her beak was scarlet.

"Who's that?" asked Hugo
and Bella together, looking up in
wonder.

Hailey felt a great thrill of
excitement and her heart began
to thump. "I think . . . I think . . . it's
the Wise Wishing Owl!" she gasped.

CHAPTER SEVEN

The Leader of
the Parade

The Wise Wishing Owl was so

beautiful that Hailey could do

nothing but stare as she glided

down into the meadow and folded her vast wings. There was silence as the fairy animals waited for her to speak.

A smile spread slowly across the owl's face. "Is everybody ready for the Christmas Parade?" she called at last. Her voice tinkled like a waterfall splashing over rocks.

"Yes!" cried all the fairy animals together. They looked at one another in delight. The Wise

Wishing Owl, the oldest and most magical creature in Misty Wood, was hardly ever seen. This was a very special day indeed.

"Would you like to lead the parade, Your Wishingness?" asked one of the Bark Badgers.

The owl shook her feathery head. "Oh, no," she said. "One of you should take the lead. I have heard much of the Christmas Parade, and so I have come here to watch."

"Then will you do us the honor of *choosing* the leader for us?" asked the Bark Badger.

"Very well." The Wise Wishing Owl looked around at all the fairy animals, her snowy-white head turning slowly from side to side.

A shiver of delight ran through Hailey as the owl's gaze fell upon her. Never in her wildest dreams had she imagined that she would have the chance to look into the deep brown eyes of the wonderful Wise Wishing Owl.

The owl furrowed her feathery brow. "It is not an easy choice," she said at last. "You all look very fine in your leaves and berries, your starshine and nutshells. But . . ." She stretched out a huge wing toward Hailey. "This little Hedgerow Hedgehog looks finer than anything I have ever seen. Will you lead the parade, my dear?"

113

Hailey gulped. She opened her mouth to reply, but no sound came out.

"Of course she will," squeaked

Bella, nodding at Hailey. "She would love to!"

Hailey took a deep breath. "Yes, I'd love to. Thank you, Wise Wishing Owl!" she cried.

"You are welcome," said the owl kindly.

"And you could start the parade off with your winter song, Hailey," Hugo piped up.

"Ooh, yes!" squealed Sabrina and Maisie.

All the fairy animals came crowding around. "We'd love to hear your song, Hailey," someone called out.

Hailey felt a tiny bit nervous, but she unfurled her wings and fluttered up above the other animals. Then she began to sing:

I love winter when the wild wind
  blows,
Scattering the leaves all around,
  all around,

Even though it chills my nose

and toes,

When I roll on the frosty ground.

As Hailey finished, her friends clapped and cheered. Hailey felt like she might burst with happiness. Then, chattering excitedly, all the fairy animals fluttered into line, ready for the Christmas Parade to begin.

The Hedgerow Hedgehogs scuttled to line up behind the

117

band. Behind them were the Bud Bunnies and the Cobweb Kittens. Then came the Holly Hamsters, the Moonbeam Moles, and the Stardust Squirrels. Behind the squirrels, the Bark Badgers marched into position. The Pollen Puppies were right at the back, yapping excitedly and running around in circles as they waited for everyone to begin moving.

"We're all ready!" cried Hailey

from high above. Light bounced off her beautiful garland and sparkled and danced all around Honeydew Meadow.

The Moss Mouse band began to play a marching song and Hailey felt her toes twitching in time to the music.

"I love winter!" she exclaimed as she headed to the front of the line. She was so happy that she did a forward roll, picking up a few

fallen leaves on her prickles.

"And I *love* Christmas even more!" she called as she uncurled again. She looked back happily at all her fairy animal friends, waiting eagerly behind her for the parade to start. "And this is the best Christmas ever!"

Turn the page for
lots of fun
Misty Wood
activities!

Connect the Dots

Follow the numbers and connect all the dots to make a lovely picture from the story. Start with dot number 1.

When you've finished connecting the dots, you can color the picture!

Winter Is Wonderful!

Hailey's favorite things about winter are colorful leaves, chestnut pudding, and the Christmas Parade!

What are your favorite things about winter? Write them down and draw a little picture of each one.

1. ....

2. ....

3. ....

Help Hugo Remember!

Hugo the Holly Hamster likes Hailey's song so much *he* wants to sing it, too! But Hugo can't remember all the words. Can you help him? Give it a try without looking back at the story!

I love winter when the wild ....
    blows,
Scattering the .... all around,
    all around,
Even though it chills my nose and
    ....,
When I roll on the frosty ....

Fairy Animals
of Misty Wood

Meet more Fairy Animal friends!

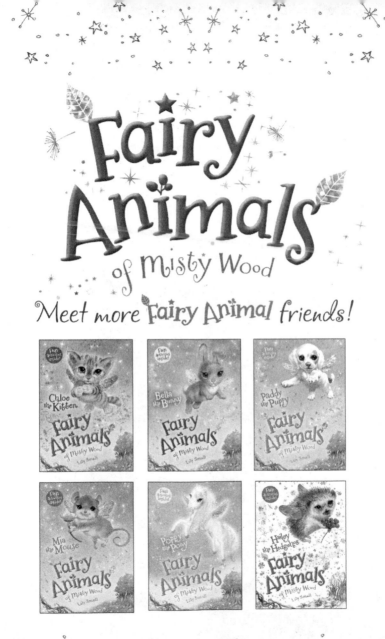